Walt Disney's
PINOCCHIO
FAVORITES

WALT DISNEY's

PINOCCHIO

FAVORITES

THE DANBURY PRESS

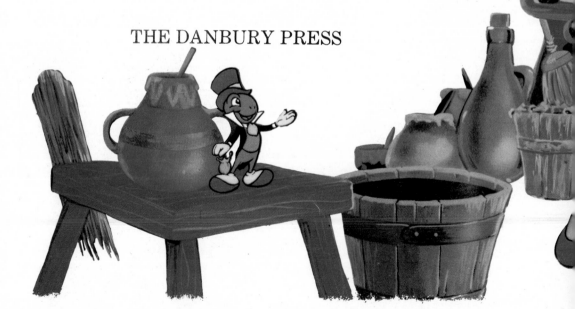

THE DANBURY PRESS

a division of Grolier Enterprises Inc.

Robert B. Clarke   *Publisher*

The Stonehouse Press   *Production Supervision*

ISBN 0–71–72–8112–4

Printed and bound in Great Britain by
Morrison & Gibb Ltd., London and Edinburgh

23456789 98765

Introduction

"Hi Diddle Dee Dee, a Writer's Life for Me." I'm Pinocchio, and I'm singing because now I have a book of my own. On these pages you'll find some of my best adventures. You'll meet J. Worthington Foulfellow (who likes to call himself Honest John . . . because he isn't) and Gideon, Geppetto, Cleo, Figaro, and my official conscience, Jiminy Cricket.

Read on and find out what it's like to be a puppet who is almost a real boy. Good reading and good fun!

Table of Contents

Geppetto's Puppet

Once upon a time in a quaint mountain village, there lived a kindly old wood-carver named Geppetto. He lived alone in his little stone house with nobody for company except Figaro the cat and Cleo the goldfish.

Even though he lived alone, Geppetto had many friends. He was always doing things for people to make them happy. The children loved him best of all because he mended their broken toys for nothing, even if he had to stop his work of carving dolls and toys. Most of the time, his shop was filled with boys and girls.

However, at night when his shop was closed and the only sound was the ticking of the clock above his bench, Geppetto was sad and lonely.

"Ah," he sighed, as he sat in his only soft chair and scratched the cat's head, "something is wrong, Figaro. During the day, when my young friends are here, I am happy. But at night, for some reason, I become sad."

Geppetto stared at the star-filled sky he could see through the window above his bed. "I think I am sad," he said slowly, "because I have no child of my own. You know something, Figaro, I would like to have a little boy, a son of my own."

Figaro half opened his eyes and meowed faintly.

"Maybe I'll make one, Figaro," said Geppetto with a small smile. "What do you say to that? Then we can both play with him. If I can make arms and legs for damaged dolls, I can certainly make a puppet."

Next morning he began carving.

Within a few days the puppet was finished. It was a handsome boy puppet, with a happy face, a red suit and a feather in its cap.

Just as Geppetto was attaching strings to it, a funny little cricket named Jiminy was passing by. He stopped to watch.

"What shall I call you?" smiled Geppetto as he played with the puppet. "I know. Since you are made of pine, I will call you Pinocchio." Jiminy edged closer to watch.

Geppetto placed the puppet carefully on a small table and looked at it sadly.

"Oh, if only you were a real boy, how happy I would be," murmured the wood-carver. Then he turned and walked slowly from the room. Jiminy felt sorry for him.

Suddenly the room was filled with a blaze of sparkles and light. The Blue Fairy appeared, touched Pinocchio with her wand and chanted, "Little puppet made of pine, awake! The gift of life is thine."

Jiminy gasped as Pinocchio began to move. The Blue Fairy smiled at Jiminy.

"Geppetto has given so much happiness to others, he deserves to have his wish come true," she said. She also told Jiminy to stay close to Pinocchio at all times. "He knows nothing of the world, so you must be his conscience." With that, she vanished.

Jiminy and Pinocchio were so excited they began to sing and dance. The noise awakened Geppetto, who rushed in to see what was happening.

"Pinocchio! You can move!" he gasped.

Geppetto was delighted. "Pinocchio, you can sing. You can dance. How did this happen?"

Jiminy explained everything. Geppetto was so happy he wept. Then, overcome with love, he gave Pinocchio a big hug.

"Ouch! Let me go! Put me down! I don't like being hugged," yelled Pinocchio.

Geppetto quickly put the puppet down.

Jiminy, seeing Pinocchio so angry, muttered, "I think I'm going to have trouble with this little wooden boy."

Figaro and Cleo thought so, too.

The Music Box

"Drip, drip, drip. Oh how I wish it would stop raining so I could go out and play," Pinocchio sighed. "What a terrible day. I've got nothing to do."

Jiminy Cricket replied, "Don't worry. The sun will come out soon. I feel it in my bones — er, my feet."

Geppetto walked in, holding a broom. "Pinocchio, my boy, would you help me sweep out my workshop? Somebody important is coming to see me, and I want it to look neat and tidy."

"I'll be happy to help you, Father," said Pinocchio, taking the broom.

When Pinocchio saw so many wood shavings, he wasn't happy about helping. "Geppetto made this mess. He should clean it up!"

"You'd better get to work, you ungrateful boy," Jiminy scolded. That made Pinocchio lose his temper.

"You can't talk to me like that!" he shouted. He swept Jiminy out of the shop into the pouring rain, then slammed the door. Jiminy was very angry and very wet.

Jiminy pounded on the door with his fists. "Let me in, Pinocchio! I'm your conscience. You can't keep me out here in the rain."

Pinocchio wouldn't answer the door. Jiminy said to himself, "I've got to get back in there. Pinocchio will get into trouble if I leave him alone." He hopped to the window ledge so he could see inside.

Jiminy was right.
Pinocchio was playing
with a pretty
carved music box
which Geppetto
was going to repair.
"I knew it!
He's headed for
trouble already,"
Jiminy shouted.

Jiminy shoved against the window, trying to get in, but it wouldn't budge. He tried to squeeze under the front door, but he was too big. He hopped up to the roof and peeked down the stovepipe that was sticking out. He grabbed one edge of the pipe and lowered himself in. "Pinoke is very clumsy. If he drops the music box, he'll ruin it."

"Yaaa-haa-haa-hooeee!" he yelled as he plummeted down the pipe.

Whomp! Bump-bump! Thud!

Jiminy bounced out of the stove and onto the floor.

C-C-C-R-A-S-H!

Pinocchio dropped the music box on the floor. Pieces of wood and metal scattered everywhere.

"Dear me, it's too late," Jiminy sighed. "Now it can never be repaired."

Hearing the crash, Geppetto came dashing in. With him was his important visitor, the man who owned the music box.

"I'm — I'm very sorry," Pinocchio sobbed.

"No, it's my fault," said Jiminy.

But the gentleman wasn't listening.

He was staring at the gold coins that lay scattered among the pieces of the music box. "What fantastic luck!" laughed the man.

"No wonder my father said the old music box was worth a lot of money. He hid his fortune in it!"

The gentleman gave Geppetto some of the gold coins and told him to make another box. Geppetto in turn gave one of the coins to Pinocchio.

By now the sun was shining, so Pinocchio ran outside to play.

Little Organ Grinder

Pinocchio was on his way to school when around a corner stepped two strangers. One was a crafty fox with shifty eyes, and the other was a dopey-looking cat.

"How do you do, young man," said the fox. "I must talk to you."

"Yeah," said the cat.

They seemed polite, but Jiminy Cricket was worried. It's not a good idea to talk to strangers, especially when you're on your way to school.

"My name is J. Worthington Foulfellow," said the fox, sweeping Jiminy out of the way with his cane. "You look like an ambitious lad. Would you like to make some money?"

"Thanks very much," replied Pinocchio, "but I can't stop. I must get to school."

"SCHOOL?" cried Foulfellow.

"Rubbish! School is for the future, but for bright lads like yourself the future is now!" The fox displayed a hand organ. "You can play this hurdy-gurdy and make a fortune."

The fox continued,
"Turn this handle
and music comes out.
People love it."
He shoved the organ
at Pinocchio.
"Stay here and
keep playing
the organ.
We'll come back
later to see
how you're doing."

The fox and the cat left Pinocchio, who stood on the sidewalk cranking the hand organ.

"Now listen here, Pinoke," said the cricket, but Pinocchio paid no attention.

"Listen, Jiminy. Isn't it pretty music?"

The fox was right about one thing. The people on the street did enjoy the music. They liked it so much they gave him coins.

Turning the handle made Pinocchio sleepy, and he dozed off. Along came a big fat rascal who had been trying to sell overripe tomatoes in the market. When he saw Pinocchio's money, he took it, leaving the rotten tomatoes in its place.

"Pinocchio! Wake up!" It was Geppetto. "Why aren't you in school?"

The wooden boy was startled. "Why, er — ah, that is, J. Worthington Foulfellow made me an offer I couldn't refuse, and . . ."

Geppetto scolded, "You naughty boy!"

While Pinocchio and Geppetto were arguing, the fox and cat returned. "Quick," said Foulfellow, "dump the money in my hat."

"Yeah," said the cat, picking up the container of money.

SQUISH!
SQUASH!
PLOOEY!

The overripe tomatoes ran down the fox's face. "Yuck! Let's get out of here!"

"I hope you've learned a lesson, Pinocchio," said Geppetto. The puppet agreed that he had.

Pinocchio Makes Friends Wherever He Travels

Pinocchio was a traveling puppet. With his friend Jiminy Cricket he visited many towns and villages, mountains and valleys. He made friends wherever he went.

One day he was traveling through a jungle when he came across a little boy his same age. The boy had never visited places like Pinocchio — in fact, he had spent all his life in the jungle. He talked to the bears and panthers and monkeys. His name was Mowgli.

The two boys became friends. Mowgli told the puppet about the ways of the jungle. Mostly the tales concerned Shere Khan, an evil tiger who hoped to get Mowgli the man-cub between his teeth and into his stomach. So far he hadn't succeeded.

The more Pinocchio thought about Mowgli and his animal friends, the more Pinocchio wanted an animal pet of his own.

The day Pinocchio met Scamp was a happy occasion. Though Scamp had no master, Pinocchio always considered the puppy as his own. He chuckled and laughed at Scamp's adventures with Lady and Tramp.

So it was that Pinocchio wanted to include stories of Mowgli and Scamp in this collection of his favorites. And as an extra bonus there are some stories of another old friend . . . Mickey Mouse.

Jungle Tree

It was dark in the jungle. The moon was out, the night was still, and Mowgli was ready to go to sleep. He stirred the ashes of his dinner fire, and old Baloo yawned.

Not far away, trouble lurked! Shere Khan was creeping silently through the bushes.

"Yum, yum," he smiled, picking his teeth with a sharpened claw, "there's Mowgli the man-cub. I've always thought he'd make a splendid meal for a certain noble tiger — me!"

Baloo yawned again. "Gosh, I'm tired, Little Britches. Time to settle down for the night."

Some of Mowgli's monkey friends were playing in the trees, and they saw the tiger. A monkey hurled a coconut at Shere Khan, and it hit his ear.

THUNK!

The monkey grinned at the tiger. "Didn't know I was watching, did you?"

"Thanks, Mr. Monkey," Mowgli said.

"It's okay. You can go to sleep now," the monkey called back.

Shere Khan slunk away, his ear hurting from the coconut and his stomach hurting from lack of dinner. He was one disappointed tiger.

Mowgli curled up
beside the fire
and went to sleep.
Baloo announced
he would
keep watch
from a tree,
but he quickly
fell asleep, too.
Before long
morning arrived.

Shere Khan awoke and stretched. He
was hungrier than ever. "I'll get that man-
cub yet," he muttered. "But how? That is
the question."

He caught sight of a large hollow tree.
He thought, "Hmmm. If bears can climb
into trees, why can't tigers?"

He tore the tree
out of the ground,
crawled inside
and began creeping
toward a jungle pond.
Mowgli was swimming
in the pond
with Bagheera.

Mowgli was having so much fun he didn't notice that a certain tree was getting closer and closer.

As Mowgli rested on a rock in the pool, he heard heavy footsteps.

THUMP! THUMP! THUMP!

Colonel Hathi was approaching.

"Hi there, Colonel," Mowgli called. "C'mon and have a drink."

"I believe I will," Hathi replied. Colonel Hathi had lived in the jungle a long time. He was no dumbbell. When he saw a tree with a tail, he knew something didn't fit. He didn't want to alarm young Mowgli, so he simply stepped on the tail as he marched to the pond.

"YIPE!" yelled the tiger.

Mowgli was very surprised to hear a tree shout.

Colonel Hathi said innocently, "Upon my word, what was that?"

The colonel, Mowgli and Bagheera all stared as the tree began running away.

"A shouting and running tree?" asked Mowgli.

"Hush now and watch," said Hathi.

Shere Khan couldn't see where he was going because the hollow trunk covered his eyes. He tripped and fell over near the top of a steep slope.

Mowgli ran forward and discovered the tiger in the tree.

Mowgli gave the tree a push and rolled Shere Khan down the slope. At the bottom were some rocks, and Shere Khan struck them hard. The hollow tree fell to pieces and there, for everyone to see, was a tiger with an aching tail, an aching head, an aching paw and a still-empty stomach.

Mowgli laughed, "Serves you right!"

The boy went back to swimming in the pond, and the tiger crawled away to lick his wounds. He muttered to himself, "If there's anything I really hate, it's a smart-aleck jungle kid."

A Good Deed

One warm afternoon Pinocchio was looking hungrily at some apples high in a tree. "Better not," said Jiminy Cricket, who knew what Pinocchio was thinking. "Those apples belong to Mrs. Jonathan. You shouldn't eat them."

"But they look so good," Pinocchio protested. With that he climbed over the stone wall and into Mrs. Jonathan's orchard. He didn't mean to do anything wrong, yet boys sometimes get hungry for juicy red apples.

"This won't do,"
Jiminy sighed.
"That boy needs
to be taught
a lesson.
You simply don't go
into an orchard and
begin eating apples."

Jiminy hopped along the road to Mrs. Jonathan's cottage. With a big smile he asked if he and his friend could pick apples for her. "We're both young and strong and good workers," he explained.

"Of course,"
she replied.
"That would be
a big help.
As you can see,
I'm much too old
to climb trees."

Jiminy borrowed a pony and cart from old Geppetto. "Be careful," Geppetto shouted from the door. "That burro isn't used to being driven by a cricket."

When Jiminy arrived back at the orchard, Pinocchio was in one of the trees looking for the biggest and best red apple in the orchard.

"As long as you're up there, pick the ripe ones and toss them into the cart," Jiminy called. "You're sure to find the best one that way."

Pinocchio liked that idea. He threw down apples as fast as he could pick them.

Before long, the cart was full, and Jiminy drove it to Mrs. Jonathan's cottage. Pinocchio had already eaten three and was about to select a fourth when Mrs. Jonathan came out of her house.

"How kind of you both!" she exclaimed. "Now you can unload the cart, and I'll give you a special reward."

Pinocchio worked hard.
His reward was
a hot apple pie
(the best he ever tasted).

Pound for Pound

Lady and Tramp were running in the park with their puppy, Scamp. "Oh, what a wonderful day to romp and play," sang Scamp. Lady warned him, "Let's all stay together."

Lady and Tramp saw their old friends, Trusty and Jock, so they stopped to talk about the weather and exchange gossip. Scamp ran ahead.

A big net flopped over Scamp. The poor puppy had been caught by the dog-catcher. Before he could utter a single sound, he was shoved inside the wagon and driven away to the pound. It looked as though Scamp might never see his parents again.

Tramp looked up in time to see Scamp peering through the bars of the wagon.

Tramp knew he had to take action, but what could he do?

At the pound the dogcatcher took Scamp out of the wagon and carried him toward a big cage where stray dogs were locked up.

In the cage were Tramp's old friends, Boris the Russian wolfhound, Peg the Pekingese, Pedro the Mexican Chihuahua, Bull the English bulldog and Dachsie the dachshund.

Boris said, "Ah, is small peasant puppy coming to join us."

"Si," added Pedro, "and eet looks like our friend Tramp, only smaller."

"Tramp?" You mean my old flame?" Peg perked her head up and looked closely at the new arrival.

The dogcatcher put Scamp in the cage.
"I'm scared," the puppy wailed.

"Is nothing to worry about, little comrade," Boris told the puppy.

"Hey," Bull asked, "do youse know a dog called Tramp?"

"Tramp? He's my daddy," Scamp replied.

"Then youse got nothing to worry about. Tramp can take care of anything," Bull continued.

"He sure can," Peg sighed.

The dogcatcher was about to lock the cage door when he heard a bark. Tramp had arrived to rescue his son.

"Another stray dog," yelled the dogcatcher. "I'll have you locked up in no time."

The man picked up his big net and ran at the dog. Tramp leaped to one side.

The man was fast, but Tramp was faster. He ran up the road with the dog-catcher after him. However, the man had forgotten to lock the cage door, and the other dogs quickly realized it.

"The door's open — that's a bit of all right," Bull shouted.

"Is freedom at last!" roared Boris.

The dogs rushed out of the cage, and Scamp followed them. They went in five different directions, and Scamp didn't know which one to follow.

Scamp's mind was soon made up for him when Tramp rushed from behind a fence and pulled Scamp to safety. "You've been in enough trouble today without scampering off after those dogs," Tramp said.

"They're my friends, and when you're older they'll be *your* friends, too. But now you belong with your mother," Tramp told Scamp. The rest of the day they played together — and *stayed* together — in the park.

Honest John Strikes Again

J. Worthington Foulfellow was back in town. Foulfellow (or Honest John, as he preferred to call himself) waited until he knew Geppetto was away from his workshop. Then, oozing charm from the tip of his black nose to the end of his bushy tail, he knocked on the door. Pinocchio and Jiminy Cricket were home alone, so the puppet answered the door.

"Good morning, young man," said Honest John Foulfellow.

"Hello," said Pinocchio. He thought a minute and scowled. "Do I know you? You look familiar."

"Oh no," said Foulfellow. "I come from a far and distant land. I am the humble servant of a wondrous king who has more money than sense."

"Oh?" said Pinocchio. He still thought he had seen this foxy fellow before.

"The king is also a clock nut. He loves clocks. We are touring your village in search of the best clocks. Do you have any?" Pinocchio led the fox to a shelf full of clocks.

The mechanical clocks went up and down, back and forth, and chimed in four languages. "Here is a cuckoo clock," said the puppet. "It costs ten dollars."

"Ten dollars?" gasped Honest John. "Why, a marvelous clock like that is worth at least *twenty*."

Pinocchio was thrilled at the idea of getting twice the price.

"My father, Geppetto, will be happy to get twenty dollars for the clock," he said, holding out his wooden hand for the money.

Honest John, however, didn't give Pinocchio any money. Instead, he told the boy, "Er — there is one small problem. Before I buy the clock, I must show it to the king. He'll know whether it will match the room and fit in with the gold and rubies and ermines and all that junk — er, all that finery."

Jiminy Cricket began hopping up and down. He recognized Honest John, and he knew that Pinocchio was being hoodwinked.

Before Jiminy could say anything, Foulfellow continued, "May I take the clock to try it out and then bring the money later?"

Jiminy hopped faster. He wanted to tell Pinocchio he would never see either the clock or the money again.

"By all means take the clock," said Pinocchio. "You can bring me the money this afternoon when you've had a chance to show the clock to the king."

"King? What king? Oh yes," — the fox caught himself before he blundered any more — "the one with all the money. I'll be back in two shakes of a fox tail."

Pinocchio and Jiminy waited and waited and waited, but Honest John didn't return. The day grew dark, and a chill wind blew down from the mountain. As the moon came out, Pinocchio had neither the clock nor the twenty dollars.

Pinocchio said, "Maybe we should go to the inn. If the king is staying there, we can ask him how he likes the clock."

They went to the local inn and asked about the king and the fox. The clerk looked down his long nose at the puppet. "King? You must be joking, little man. There is no king within two hundred miles of this village."

Pinocchio tried to explain.

"No more of your sassy talk. There is no king here. Off with you. Begone."

The doorman at the inn overheard their conversation and took pity on Pinocchio. "I think I know that foxy Foulfellow," he said.

"He never stays here — he's too cheap. He camps in a grove outside town. I'll take you there."

They walked to the grove, and there was Honest John cooking his dinner. Pinocchio said, "I want my clock back."

"Clock? I have no clock," said the fox. "I've never seen you before, and I haven't been near Geppetto's all day."

It seemed
there was nothing
Pinocchio could do.
Maybe the fox
had already sold
the clock
to somebody else,
and Pinocchio
would never
get it back.
Suddenly there
was a noise!

CUCKOO! CUCKOO! CUCKOO!

The clock struck the hour and burst out of the package. The fox was caught with the goods, and he couldn't talk his way out of it.

After thanking the doorman for his help, Pinocchio and Jiminy grabbed the clock and took it home. They hoped they would never see Foulfellow again.

But it was not to be. The following week he was back, this time with his assistant, Gideon. The fox and the cat were at the carnival. They were offering a basket of strawberries to the person who came closest to guessing how many jelly beans were in a glass jar.

"I'll guess!" Pinocchio called. "I'll guess there are 200 jelly beans."

"Very good," said the fox. "You give me a dime for your guess, and at five o'clock under the town clock I will give the strawberries to the winner."

Jiminy guessed that the fox was up to no good, but he couldn't make Pinocchio listen. Jiminy decided to take matters into his own hands.

All afternoon, while Pinocchio was playing games or riding rides along the carnival midway, Jiminy kept an eye on Honest John and Gideon.

At four o'clock he followed them as they slipped away from the carnival and crept into a dark alley. There they counted all the dimes.

"Over nine dollars," grinned the fox. "How nice. Now we will run away with the money and keep the strawberries for our dinner. Nobody will look for us before five o'clock."

Jiminy was astounded at what he heard. He yelled, "Stop, thieves! Stop!"

Unhappily,
no honest citizen
was near enough
to hear Jiminy.
Honest John and
Gideon laughed.

Finally Gideon picked up the cricket and tied him to a balloon. "Float away, little nuisance," sneered the fox, "and let us steal our money in peace."

Up, up, up into the air floated the cricket and the balloon.

However, if Jiminy was unlucky that no-body heard him, he was lucky now. Pinocchio was trying to climb the carnival's greased pole. He had tried every other game or ride, and now he was inching up the pole. Jiminy floated nearby. "Help, Pinocchio," he squeaked.

The puppet reached out a hand and grab-bed at Jiminy. His hand was greasy, and Jiminy slipped through. He tried once more as the cricket drifted past. He missed Jiminy again but got the string.

Pinocchio released his hold on the pole, and puppet and cricket together sped quickly earthward.

Pinocchio ran through the carnival midway and down the street to the police station. Soon a policeman went with them to arrest J. Worthington Foulfellow and Gideon. He took them to jail.

There, behind bars,
the fox and the cat
had to count jelly beans
and announce the winner.
Guess who won!
That's right — Pinocchio!

Pinocchio took the strawberries home to share them with Jiminy and Geppetto. The three of them ate extra helpings of strawberry shortcake while Honest John and Gideon munched dry bread and water.

"Honesty always pays," Geppetto said after dinner, "and those two scoundrels are getting what they deserve. Act properly, Pinocchio, and always let your conscience be your guide."

Jiminy added, "Especially when your conscience is a cricket."

Goofy's Dinner Party

Brrring! Brrring! Mickey Mouse's telephone was ringing. He picked it up and said, "Hello."

"Hi, Mick. This is Goofy. I want you to come over for dinner tonight. You're always doing me favors, so I thought I'd do something nice for you."

"Thanks," said Mickey. "That sounds great."

Mickey got ready for dinner. He knew it would be something special, so he put on his best suit and a new shirt and tie.

He walked to Goofy's house.

Swoosh! A shower of water shot over Mickey.

"Sorry," said Goofy, putting down the garden hose. "I was watering the yard so it would look nice for you."

"Never mind," said Mickey, trying not to worry about his good suit.

Mickey stepped inside. Whizz! Crash! He slid on a rug and skidded down the hall.

"Gorsh, I'm sorry," said Goofy. "I polished the floor especially for you."

By this time Goofy was so nervous he offered Mickey some lemonade and spilled it down Mickey's shirt.

He spent so long wiping up the lemonade that the steak burned.

Mickey looked at the pile of ashes that was once a piece of meat.

"I guess it's a little overdone," said Goofy.

Mickey rubbed his bumps and bruises. "Oh, it's fine, but I just remembered that I'm expecting an important phone call from Alaska. I'd better get home. Thanks for the party. It was wonderful."

"Glad you enjoyed yourself," said Goofy. Come again, any time."

Pinocchio's Snowman

One morning Pinocchio awoke to hear a
faint rustling outside his bedroom window.
He crawled out of his warm bed to see what
it was. "Maybe it's a bird trying to get in,"
he thought. What he saw were small flecks
of white beating against the windowpane.
Suddenly he knew what it was. "Snow!" he
cried. "It's snowing outside."

A soft blanket of snow covered the ground. Pinocchio's eyes sparkled with excitement. "Oh boy, am I going to have fun today! I'll throw snowballs and make snowmen and play with my sled." By the time he was dressed, Pinocchio had his whole day planned.

Downstairs, Geppetto asked, "What are you doing dressed? When you get up you always have a warm bath first."

"Not today," Pinocchio answered.

Pinocchio opened the front door. Geppetto called, "Wait, what about your breakfast and your bath?" Pinocchio ran outside.

"Fiddlesticks," Pinocchio shouted from outside. "I hate baths. All they do is clean you up. And I'm not hungry. I'm going to play in the snow and make myself a snowman."

He threw snowballs, slid on the ice and began packing snow for a statue.

Jiminy Cricket watched from a tree branch. "You're a bad boy," Jiminy yelled. "You didn't obey your father. You should have eaten breakfast and taken a warm bath."

Pinocchio laughed,
"You only want
to spoil my fun,
Jiminy. I won't
listen to you."
He threw a snowball
at Jiminy,
who jumped away
in the nick of time.
Jiminy shook
his umbrella.
"If I were bigger,
I'd spank you."

"Don't be mad, Jiminy" Pinocchio said. "Why don't you help me make a snowman instead?"

"Make it yourself!" snapped Jiminy.

"All right, I will."

Pinocchio set to work, and in two hours he had built a huge snowman. He stood before it and admired his wonderful creation.

By now it was warmer. Snow was beginning to melt, and icicles dripped steadily on the paths and walkways.

"That's the biggest snowman in the world," Pinocchio said proudly. "How do you like it, Jimin —" Pinocchio never finished the word. His snowman began to topple over.

SPLOSH!

The snowman fell right on Pinocchio.

"Splutter! Koff-koff!" Pinocchio was coughing and shivering as he pulled himself out of the snow. He was wet clear through.

"Serves you right," Jiminy told him. "You didn't get a nice warm bath — you got a nice *cold* bath."

Jungle Giant

Mowgli was pleased with himself. He found that by knocking two empty coconut halves together, he could make a clip-clop noise that sounded like footsteps.

"I must have old Baloo hear this," he chuckled. "He'll think it's fun." He hurried off to find the big bear.

Not far from Mowgli his enemy, Shere Khan, lurked in the underbrush.

The wicked tiger was prowling around, looking for lunch. He hadn't found anything tasty to eat, and he was hungry. When he heard the clip-clopping he smiled greedily and smacked his lips.

He slunk through the bushes where his stripes made him almost invisible. From his hiding place he saw Mowgli marching along, banging the coconut shells together.

"I think man-cub would make a fine addition to my royal stomach," the tiger said.

The tiger crouched lower. "He'll be difficult to catch, so I'll use extra cunning. I'll play a waiting game."

Mowgli was walking straight toward Shere Khan's hiding place when who should come out of the forest but Baloo!

"Hi there, old papa bear," said Mowgli. "Listen to this sound."

"Hey, man, that's wild," said Baloo. "That's out of sight. The greatest. Hold on a minute while I get myself another one of those crazy coconuts."

Nearby was a coconut palm with some ripe nuts on it.

"You can climb that tree over there and get a coconut," said Mowgli, pointing.

"Aw, not today. I'm a tired old bear this morning. I'll shag a rock at it instead."

Baloo hunted around, found a rock and tossed it at the tree. Not only was the bear tired, his aim was tired, too. It didn't come close to the tree. It sailed wide of the mark.

Mowgli laughed. "Nowhere near. You couldn't hit the broad side of an alligator at ten paces."

"Well now,
at that rate
I'll never make
the Jungle Giants
softball team,"
Baloo admitted.

Though the rock didn't hit a coconut, it did hit something else. It landed against a hornets' nest hanging from the branch of another tree. The hornets were angry at having their lunch interrupted and their home knocked down.

PLOP!
The nest fell
smack on the head
of Shere Khan.
What a shock!
What's worse,
the hornets blamed
the tiger!

The hornets
attacked and
stung the tiger.
"OW--ooo--AH!"
roared Shere Khan.
He dashed
into the jungle.

Bagheera, alerted by Shere Khan's howls, asked, "What's the matter with our lordly tiger?"

Baloo bragged, "Well, I knew he was hiding there, waiting for Mowgli, so I threw a rock at a hornets' nest. They chased him away and saved us the trouble."

Mowgli was surprised. "Baloo, you didn't know Shere Khan was there. You were aiming at the coconuts and missed."

"How can you doubt me?" Baloo asked. "Me, the best pitcher the Jungle Giants ever had? I don't miss by that much. I was only kidding you."

Bagheera, who knew Baloo well enough to know he was trying to save face, suggested they all have lunch. Mowgli ate the coconuts, but Baloo said, "I think I'll make the clip-clop sounds instead. I've got to watch my diet if I'm going back into training."

The Lost Ball

"You have been a good boy lately," said Geppetto to Pinocchio, "and you deserve a reward. Here is a new bat and ball."

"Oh thank you," Pinocchio answered. "Now I can play ball like the real boys do. C'mon, Jiminy, let's have some fun."

Playing ball with a cricket was not easy, but Pinocchio made the best of it. "You pitch, Jiminy, and I'll hit," he said.

"Okay, but don't hit the ball too hard."

Jiminy Cricket
tossed the ball.
Pinocchio took
a big, full swing.
The ball soared
high in the air.

The ball dropped neatly into the top of a tall, hollow tree. Jiminy sighed, "You should have remembered my warning and not hit the ball so hard. We'll never get your ball. It's lost forever."

They both sat quietly and stared at
the hollow tree, trying to figure out a
way to get the ball. Finally Jiminy said,
"Geppetto will be hurt when he hears that
you've lost your new ball. Why don't you
do something helpful to make up for it?"

"That's a fine idea," replied Pinocchio.
"I'll water the yard." He got the hose and
sprayed water over most of the yard and
over all of Jiminy.

Pinocchio then had an idea.

He aimed the hose so the water poured into the top of the hollow tree. Soon the trunk was full of water, and floating on top was his ball. When the water flowed over the top of the tree, the ball rolled out.

"Good thinking," cried Jiminy. "I knew there was more in your head than just wood."

"Hooray!" shouted Pinocchio. "Now we can play ball again."

Siamese Brats

It was a warm spring day, and bossy Aunt Sarah had come to visit. As if Aunt Sarah weren't enough, she brought her two Siamese cats with her.

The cats, whose names were Si and Am, went to work on everything in sight. They sharpened their claws on an antique chair, a brand new coffee table and the newly-painted dining room walls. What's worse, Scamp got the blame.

Tramp called them Siamese *brats*.

Whenever Aunt Sarah came into the room, the two cats purred and rubbed against her legs. She couldn't believe her darlings would do any damage, so she threw Scamp out of the house.

Three times!

Tramp didn't say anything to Scamp — after all, learning about cats was part of growing up. But when he saw them clawing up a new embroidered pillow, he told Lady, "It's time I had a word with those cats."

He jumped through the window, much to the surprise of Si and Am. A moment later it was Tramp who was in trouble. Both he and the cushion went sliding across the floor. CRASH! A hat stand tipped over, hats flying in every direction.

Aunt Sarah saw it all. "I'll teach you to frighten my poor cats," she cried.

She grabbed the dog by the collar and dragged him to the cupboard. Then she phoned the dog pound.

Si and Am heard it all, and they ran to tell Lady, snickering to themselves all the while. When they finished, Scamp said, "Don't believe them, Mother. Dad wouldn't let himself get caught."

For once the cats were telling the truth, for along the road came the dogcatcher in his wagon.

"Dad will find
a way to escape,"
Scamp said,
but his mother
wasn't so sure.

Tramp had escaped from the best dog
pounds in the county, so a little cupboard
wasn't going to hold him. A jiggle here, a
jounce there, a jot of pressure in the right
place, and the door sprang open.

Tramp was free!

The dogcatcher was unlatching the back door
of his wagon when out of the house raced Tramp.
Right behind him was Aunt Sarah. "Catch him!"
the woman shouted to the dogcatcher. "Hurry and
catch that awful dog!"

The dogcatcher began chasing Tramp.

The two Siamese cats, who had come out to
gloat, didn't know that the door to the wagon
was open.

Boris said, "Is two cats from the aristocracy.
Is best to chase them."

"Righto," said Bull. "Nothing beats chasing a stuck-up cat, I always say."

YEEOWL!

All the dogs in the wagon escaped through the open door and raced after Si and Am.

The two cats streaked down the road, with the dogs after them. Behind the dogs was Aunt Sarah.

Scamp wanted to join in the fun, but Tramp said it was best not to.

Later that day Scamp, Lady and Tramp watched Aunt Sarah pack her bags and leave. With her went Si and Am. "I'm never coming back again," Aunt Sarah declared.

"That's soon enough for me," Tramp whispered to Scamp. "Cats are all right in their place, and their place is far away from us dogs."

Out West

Mickey Mouse and Goofy were visiting a dude ranch west of the Pecos. They dressed up in sombreros and chaps and had toy cap pistols in their belts.

One day they were riding along the trail when they noticed some corn on the ground. "Somebody ahead of us must be driving a cart with sacks of corn on it," said Mickey, "and one sack must be leaking."

Soon they saw the cart. They saw something else, too — two badmen were robbing the man on the cart.

"What can we do to help?" asked Goofy.

"We'll use the corn to stop those bad guys," said Mickey. He told Goofy how.

A few minutes later, Mickey walked up to the robbers. "Okay," he said. "Drop those guns."

The badmen looked at Mickey and laughed. "Hah! What can a little twerp like you do?"

"Not just me," said Mickey. "Me and my men."

"What men?"

"I've got a posse hiding in the rocks."

A badman sneered, "I don't see any men."

"That's because they're hiding. I'm gonna give an order to shoot in the air. Then if you don't give

me your guns, they'll shoot *at* you instead of *over* you."

"I don't believe you," said the other badman.

Mickey called, "Okay, fellas, shoot."

Bang! Bang! Bang! The air was full of gunshots. The two badmen threw down their guns.

Goofy came down from the rocks. He was doing what he liked best — eating popcorn. "Gorsh, Mick, it was a pretty good idea of yours, roasting all that dropped corn so it popped like gunshots."

"Just brains over brawn," said Mickey.

Cleaning the Path

One morning Geppetto awoke and looked out his bedroom window. He saw that it had snowed hard all night and that snowdrifts were everywhere.

"The path to my shop will have to be cleaned off. I'll have Pinocchio do it so that I can go on with my work," he said.

He took Pinocchio outside and showed him a shovel. "The walk must be cleared of snow so that people won't fall and hurt themselves. And I want you to do it."

Then Geppetto took a shiny coin out of his pocket and handed it to the puppet. "This is for you. When you have finished, you can spend it on anything you want."

Pinocchio looked
at the coin.
"Oh boy, now I
can buy a big bag
of candy mints."
He dropped
the shovel
and ran down
the path,
intending to go
to the candy store.

As he reached the gate he slipped and fell
headfirst into the snow. KER-PLOP! The coin
flew out of his hand toward Jiminy Cricket,
who was standing on the gatepost. Pinocchio
raised his head out of the snow, looked at
Jiminy and asked, "What happened?"

"You slipped because you were in a hurry to get out of doing what you were supposed to do." Jiminy frowned as he spoke.

"Where's my money? I don't see it."

Pinocchio noticed Jiminy holding something behind his back. "You've got it," he laughed. "Give it back."

"Pinocchio," Jiminy said sternly, "you received this coin to clear the snow off the path. You must do that first."

"Fiddlesticks!" Pinocchio snapped.

"If you feel that way, then you don't deserve the money." With those words, Jiminy flipped the coin over Pinocchio's head. It landed in the snow and disappeared from sight. Jiminy said, "If you want it, you'll have to dig for it."

Pinocchio ran to get the shovel.

He started shoveling snow in all directions.
Only after the entire path had been cleared
did Pinocchio find his coin.

Geppetto was proud of his boy and con-
gratulated him, but Pinocchio admitted, "I
shouldn't take all the credit. Jiminy helped."

Pinocchio winked at Jiminy — they both
understood.

All That Glitters Is Not Gold

One fine day J. Worthington Foulfellow and Gideon the cat came sneaking into town. With them they brought a large, glittering, gold-colored brick. "What a perfect day for cheating somebody," the fox said with a wink. "Now whom shall it be?"

At that moment Pinocchio strolled down the street with Jiminy Cricket.

Foulfellow breezed up to the puppet. "Ah, what a nice little boy. Do you happen to have a hundred dollars on you?"

Pinocchio burst out laughing. "A hundred dollars? Of course not!"

"Pity," sighed the fox. He held up the gold brick, which glistened in the sunlight. "This gold brick is worth two hundred, but since you are such a fine lad, I'll sell it to you for one hundred. A real bargain."

"Yeah," said Gideon.

Pinocchio's eyes grew large.

"I would like
to buy the brick,"
said Pinocchio.
"It looks like
a smart purchase.
But —"

"At the moment," Foulfellow interrupted, "I am so hungry, I will exchange this valuable brick for a good dinner."

Pinocchio knew that Geppetto had already started cooking dinner at home. He broke into a happy smile. "It's a deal," he cried.

Jiminy was afraid Pinocchio was going to do something foolish. He chased after the boy, trying to warn him, but Pinocchio paid no attention.

Pinocchio ran in the house and filled a dish with potatoes that were baking in the embers and a big, turkey drumstick. As an extra bonus

he took a pair of shoes for the barefoot cat.

Jiminy was very angry. "No," he cried. "You are making a big mistake."

Pinocchio was sure the cricket was wrong. He rushed outside with the dinner and the shoes.

"An excellent bargain," the sly fox proclaimed as he gave Pinocchio the gold brick. "You are exactly the kind of lad I'd hoped to meet. A smart lad like yourself should grow up to be president or mayor or something."

Geppetto, who was upstairs, heard the conversation and looked out the window to see what was going on. He recognized the fox, and he dashed down the stairs and out the back door to get the police.

"You've done the wrong thing —
again," Jiminy wailed as he followed
Pinocchio into the house.

Pinocchio tripped on the doorstep.
The gold brick went flying out of his
hands.

KER-RASH!

The brick hit the floor and broke
into a thousand pieces.

Pinocchio's brick was made of clay.
The puppet stared at the pieces
and knew he'd been a fool!

He felt awful because he'd given the fox and the cat Geppetto's dinner and shoes for nothing!

Then he saw the wood-carver coming in with the food and the shoes. "Cheer up." Geppetto said with a gentle smile. "I saw what those scoundrels were doing, and I called the police. They recovered my shoes and our dinner."

In the background they could hear the fox talking to the policeman. "Ah, a wise man like yourself can surely see that a man of my character could never stoop to selling a gold brick —" The policeman was having none of it. He took the fox and the cat off to jail.

Geppetto assured Pinocchio, "You have learned an important lesson. When somebody offers you a great deal for very little, always suspect a trick. Now let's eat dinner."

The Girl Friend

Pinocchio rubbed his eyes and took a good look. Yes, it was a girl, all right. But what was she doing here in Geppetto's shop?

"I want you to meet my niece," said Geppetto. "Her name is Gretel. I'm going to be busy today, and I thought the two of you could play together."

"Well, okay," said the wooden boy.

He whispered
to Jiminy Cricket,
"Little boys
don't like
little girls.
I don't want
to play with her.
But I've got
a secret plan."

He turned to Gretel. "Come on, and I'll take you for a boat ride on the lake."

Jiminy was uneasy. "I'd better keep an eye on Pinocchio or he'll get into trouble."

Down at Pine Tree Lake, Gretel
picked out the rowboat she liked best,
and Pinocchio rented it from the
boatman.

"Let me help you into the boat,"
offered Pinocchio.

Gretel smiled and said, "How kind
of you."

Next Jiminy hopped in.

But Pinocchio had no intention of
getting into the boat.

"Take your boat ride with Jiminy," he shouted. With that, he put one foot on the boat and pushed it away from the stone pier. But he pushed too hard. The boat shot away, and Pinocchio lost his balance.

SPLASH! Pinocchio went under water and came up sputtering.

"Poor Pinocchio," said Gretel. "You're all wet and dirty."

The wooden boy stood up. Slick mud ran down his face and covered his clothes. He sobbed, "Geppetto will be angry. He doesn't like to wash clothes, and I don't know how."

"Don't worry," said Gretel. I'll wash your clothes for you. I don't want you to get into trouble. I can tell you're really a good boy, even though you are made of wood."

Gretel washed and rinsed
the clothes in the lake.
Soon they were as clean as new.

"Thanks, Gretel. Now Geppetto won't be angry because I got them dirty." Jiminy asked, "Now what are you going to do, Pinocchio?"

Pinocchio replied, "I am going to play with Gretel." They ran home, and Pinocchio got out his new ball.

As it turned out, Gretel was a good volleyball player, especially with a purple volleyball. Geppetto was happy to see how well they were getting along.

Pinocchio decided that little boys could like little girls, especially if they were good at washing clothes.

Mickey—
Master Painter

"Gorsh, Mickey, that looks keen," Goofy said.

He was looking at Mickey's car. Mickey was putting the finishing touches on a new paint job. Instead of being blue, the car now had bright red and white stripes.

Mickey wiped off his brush. "Stripes are the fashion this year. Some cars have racing stripes that go back and forth, but I wanted my car to have stripes going up and down."

"Would you mind if I painted my car with stripes like yours?" Goofy asked.

"Not at all. Be my guest."

Mickey didn't see Goofy for the rest of the day. He didn't see him the next day, either. But the morning after that, Goofy knocked at Mickey's door.

Mickey was surprised when he opened the door and saw Goofy. His friend was worn out. "Gosh, what have you been doing?" Mickey asked.

"I'm so tired," Goofy answered. "I've been to every paint shop in town. I even went to paint shops

in other towns. No matter where I went, I couldn't get any paint like you used for your car."

Goofy kicked off his shoes and rubbed his aching feet. "I don't like to bother you again, Mickey, but please tell me where you bought that paint."

"At the hardware store at the corner."

Goofy frowned. "Gorsh, I went there first. The guy told me he didn't have any paint like that."

"What kind of paint did you ask for, Goofy?"

"Why, the same as yours. I asked for a can of red and white striped paint!"

Bad Luck Turns Good

Pinocchio and Jiminy Cricket went for a walk in the village. In front of Mr. Rizzoti's pie shop they found a horseshoe.

"Throw it over your shoulder, and it will bring you good luck," said Jiminy.

Pinocchio picked up the horseshoe. "It's big. It should bring us a big fortune."

Pinocchio threw the horseshoe.

Jiminy said, "Oh no — not in that direction!" But he was too late.

The horseshoe went through the front window of the pie shop. The pie man was angry. "Look what you've done! You will have to pay for that broken window," he said, grabbing Pinocchio by the ear.

Pinocchio agreed to pay, and Mr. Rizzoti let go of his ear. But Pinocchio had no money. What would he do?

He asked Jiminy,
"Where will I
get the money
for Mr. Rizzoti?"
Jiminy answered,
"Where there's
a will,
there's a way."
They continued
down the street.

There were some boys playing ball in a field. Pinocchio wanted to join them, but he was too worried to enjoy a game.

"A pin!" Jiminy cried, pointing to a pin on the ground. "See a pin and pick it up, and all the day you'll have good luck."

"Bah!" said Pinocchio. "I'm through with your silly advice."

"See a pin and let it lay," Jiminy continued, "bad luck you'll have the rest of the day."

A big ball whizzed over the fence, bounced on Pinocchio's head and plopped into a pond.

Jiminy said, "If you had bent down to pick up the pin, the ball wouldn't have hit you on the head."

A boy ran from the playground and said, "That's our ball. Since it bounced off your head and into the water, you get it back."

The boys were bigger than Pinocchio, so he did what they said.

Pinocchio got
a stick and
tried to reach
the ball.
SPLASH!
He fell
into the water.

He sank to the bottom of the pond and saw something bright and shiny there. He grabbed it. When he got to the surface, he bounced the ball to the boys and then studied the shiny thing in his hand.

"It's a gold charm bracelet," he said.
"I'll take it to the police station."

The police sergeant said there was a reward for returning the bracelet, and it was enough to pay for Mr. Rizzoti's window and buy ice cream for his friends.

"Have you another saying?" he asked Jiminy as he licked his ice cream cone.

"What about, 'Honesty always pays'?"

"It certainly paid me," Pinocchio said, laughing.

Scamp Meets Trusty

Scamp was sitting with Lady and Tramp at the gate to their yard one afternoon. They saw a big dog coming their way, with his nose down, sniffing the ground.

"Who's that dog?" asked Scamp. "Why does he keep his nose on the ground like that?"

"That's old Trusty the bloodhound," replied Tramp. "He goes around sniffing the ground because he's lost his sense of smell, and he's trying to find it. At least that's what Jock the Scotty says."

Trusty ambled past them, not speaking.

Scamp watched him as he walked off. "Gee, I hope Mr. Trusty finds his smell," he said.

"I'm sure he will," smiled Lady.

Scamp yawned. "Well, I'm going to find a shady spot and take a nap."

"I'll go in the house," said Lady. "Coming, Scamp?"

"No," replied the puppy. "I'll stay outside with Dad."

But Scamp couldn't sleep. He kept think-

ing about poor old Trusty and his lost sense of smell. When Trusty came sniffing by again, Scamp jumped up and spoke to him.

"Mr. Trusty, can I help you find your smell?"

Trusty looked up. "Waal now, that's mighty nice of you," he drawled. "But are you allowed out by yourself?"

"I won't be by myself if I'm with you," returned Scamp.

Trusty thought it over. "Guess that's right." He resumed sniffing, with Scamp trotting alongside him.

A few minutes later Lady realized Scamp was missing. She woke up Tramp, and the two of them began searching for their puppy.

Jock the Scotty ran into the yard. "I saw Scamp with Trusty a little while ago. They seemed to be looking for something."

At that moment Trusty returned, still sniffing. He had no idea where Scamp was. "He was here a minute ago," he admitted.

"Fine bloodhound *you* are," Jock grumbled. "First you lose your sense of smell, and then you lose the wee pup!"

Tramp hurried down the block. As he passed some drainpipes on the street, he heard a faint yipping. It came from inside one of the pipes. "Scamp, is that you?" called Tramp.

"Yes, Dad. I didn't watch where I was going and got stuck in the pipe. I can't get out because there's something prickly in the way."

Tramp barked into the pipe, telling Scamp to back out. Just then a small boy came around the corner and saw Tramp.

"Hi, Tramp," said the boy. "Have you found Henry?"

Tramp wondered exactly who Henry was.

"Stand back, Tramp," the boy ordered. He lifted one end of the pipe.

Out tumbled Scamp. He was followed by a round object covered with prickly spines.

"That's Henry! He's my pet porcupine!" said the boy.

The boy picked up Henry — very carefully. "Wait here," he said to the dogs. "I'll be right back." A minute later he returned with a big bone. He said, "Here's a reward for finding Henry. I'm sorry there's only one bone for all you nice dogs."

The dogs agreed that Scamp should have the bone, but the puppy gave it to Trusty. "If it hadn't been for Trusty, I wouldn't have gone into the pipe."

Trusty accepted the bone, explaining, "When I get back my sense of smell, I'll find you the biggest bone in the world."

Pinocchio Gets The Bird

One bright summer day Pinocchio and Jiminy Cricket went for a walk in the country. They were nearing a small meadow when they heard two boys shouting and yelling. As Pinocchio got nearer he saw the boys wrestling and punching each other.

"I don't like their looks," Jiminy warned. "They're the kind of boys who like to fight, and you don't want to get hurt."

As usual, Pinocchio didn't listen. He went up to the boys and said politely, "My name is Pinocchio, and I like to play baseball and football. May I play with you?"

"Haw! Did you hear that, Eddie? This funny kid wants to play with us."

"That's a laugh," roared Eddie.

"What's so funny about me?" Pinocchio demanded. "I'm a boy just like you."

"If you're like us," said Eddie slyly, "you could climb this tree and steal a bird's egg. Right, Hank?"

"Yeah," said Hank with a crooked grin. "Let's see you steal an egg. The nest is in that hole up there." He pointed upward.

Pinocchio gulped when he saw how high he would have to climb. "I'll do it," he said. "Right now."

Jiminy took Pinocchio aside. "Don't do it," he urged. "You shouldn't steal a mama bird's eggs."

Pinocchio paid no attention and began climbing. He had to struggle to reach the hole. Suddenly out popped a rare and angry giant red-headed, green-bellied, yellow-winged longbeak. Pinocchio was frightened.

Eddie and Hank rolled on the ground with laughter. The rare and angry giant longbeak bit Pinocchio on the nose, and the boys laughed even harder. Silly Pinocchio — he didn't realize the two boys knew there was a bird in the hole all the time!

"What a dunce! He fell for the joke."

Pinocchio, trying to get away from the rare and angry longbeak, slipped. Down he fell, landing on top of Eddie and Hank.

CU-RUNCH!

"What's the big idea?" Eddie yelled at Hank. "I don't like guys falling on me."

Hank shouted, "It was your idea — you sent the kid up there."

"I'll show you."

Eddie punched Hank in the nose as Jiminy tried to pull Pinocchio away. Hank hit Eddie back, and the two fell to the ground fighting each other.

Pinocchio said, "Let's go, Jiminy. You were right. But I didn't get hurt, *they* did!"

The Foolish Boast

As Pinocchio and Jiminy Cricket walked down the street they saw some boys and girls playing with a jump rope. Pinocchio exclaimed, "That looks like fun. I'll bet I can jump and skip rope better than any of them."

"Are you sure?" Jiminy warned. "You shouldn't brag about doing things you haven't tried."

Before Pinocchio could answer, the children were inviting him to join their game.

A little boy asked,
"Would you like us
to teach you
to jump rope?"
"No," said Pinocchio.
The little boy said,
"Are you sure you can jump
without falling down?"

"Of course I can," Pinocchio boasted. "I can skip better than you!"

Poor Pinocchio! The first time he tried to jump over the rope, it caught him around one ankle and then the other. He fell on his face and got slivers in his splinters.

"Serves you right," Jiminy said while the children laughed. "You were boasting again."

Pinocchio didn't like being laughed at. "That game is too easy." He stomped off.

Jiminy warned,
"If you are
a poor loser,
they won't invite
you to play again."
Pinocchio sniffed,
"I don't care."

Pinocchio started down the street. "They laughed at me when I fell down."

"Stop feeling sorry for yourself," said Jiminy. "It's better to make folks laugh than cry."

Pinocchio knew the cricket was right.

"All right,"
Pinocchio said,
"I was foolish.
Let's go back
and I'll learn
to jump rope
properly."
They hurried back.

The street was empty —
the children were gone
but the rope was there.
Pinocchio picked it up.

Jiminy tried to help Pinocchio skip rope,
but he wasn't very good at it.

Suddenly Mrs. Sassafras came rushing
down the street. She saw Pinocchio with
the rope. "So *you* are the naughty boy who
stole my clothesline! I'll teach you not to
be naughty again!" She grabbed Pinocchio
by the ear, picked up the clothesline and
marched him to her house.

Mrs. Sassafras made Pinocchio tie up the line and hang out the laundry. She warned him that if he dropped anything, she would make him wash it again.

Not until the laundry was hanging on the line did she let Pinocchio go. When he reached the street, the boys and girls were waiting for him.

"We're sorry you got into trouble for something we did," they said. "We want to make it up to you for taking our punishment for us."

Pinocchio knew the boys and girls were really sorry. "All right," he said brightly, "let's all play together." "What shall we play?" they asked.

"Anything!" Pinocchio answered. "Just as long as it isn't jumping rope — I'm not very good at that, I guess."

Jiminy saw that one boy had a large soccer ball. "I'll roll the ball to you, and you kick it," the cricket said. "I can catch better than anything."

Jiminy rolled the ball, and Pinocchio kicked it high over the cricket's head.

"Now look who's boasting," Pinocchio laughed, and the children laughed with him.

Surprise Party

Goofy had a large apple tree growing in his back yard. There were always so many apples that he couldn't eat them all, so each year Goofy had a Happy Apple-Eating Party. Everyone came over and picked apples, and afterwards they stayed and played.

This year things were different. Goofy's friends arrived to pick apples as usual. Morty and Ferdie climbed high into the tree, but instead of staying to play pirate or explorer, they climbed down and skipped off somewhere else. Clarabelle and Minnie and Daisy all left early.

By noon the party was over. The house was quiet. There were no joyful noises of friends having fun.

Goofy was hungry, so he went outside to pick himself an apple. There were no more apples on the tree. It was bare.

Tired and hungry, Goofy sat down under his apple tree. He was very discouraged and disappointed. He thought, "My friends have all changed."

He awoke later because his nose was smelling hot

apple pie with cinnamon. He went into the kitchen.

"Surprise!" yelled Goofy's friends.

Mickey Mouse explained, "You're always so gener-
ous with us, we thought you should enjoy your apples,
too. So we hurried home to fix you some cider, turn-
overs, pies, preserves and all sorts of goodies."

Clarabelle Cow said, "Instead of having the apples
only one day, now you can enjoy them all winter
long."

"Golly," said Goofy. "I don't know what to say."

"I do," said Mickey. "Let's eat!"

Keeping Snowy White

"Pinocchio, the reason you never do the right thing is that you always think of yourself first. You should begin thinking of others."

Jiminy Cricket was hopping alongside Pinocchio as the little puppet walked down a country lane. "Like today," Jiminy continued. "There were chores to do at home, but you've gone for a walk instead."

"Not a walk, Jiminy. I want to visit my friend Snowy," Pinocchio answered.

Snowy was a big, white, furry, fluffy dog that belonged to Mrs. Floomis. "Hi, Mrs. Floomis, can I take Snowy for a walk?" Pinocchio asked.

"Snowy would like that," the woman said. "But please see that he doesn't get dirty. He's just had a bath, and there are many puddles in the fields."

"Don't worry,"
Pinocchio replied.
"Jiminy and I
will keep Snowy
extra clean."
The three of them
hurried off
down the lane.

Keeping a large white dog snowy clean was not easy. A farm wagon trundled past. Bump-bump-splash! One of its wheels hit a muddy puddle.

Pinocchio jumped in front of Snowy. The dog was still clean, but the wooden boy's clothes were a mess. His red pants were caked with mud, and his yellow shirt was wet clear through.

Jiminy had an idea.

"We should know better than to walk along a muddy road," he said. "Let's go across the meadow." Snowy liked the idea and tugged at his leash.

The dog spied a rabbit and raced after it, dragging Pinocchio and Jiminy through tall grass and bushes and hedges.

"Don't let go," yelled Jiminy. "We can't let Snowy get dirty."

"I wish we hadn't taken this dog for a walk," Pinocchio panted. "It's all I can do to keep up with him." The rabbit jumped across a creek.

Snowy crossed the water by neatly hopping from one stepping stone to another. He didn't get wet. Pinocchio, who was being dragged behind, splashed through the water. He was soaked!

The rabbit ran into a hole, so Snowy lost interest. Instead, he found a muddy field and romped toward it.

"We can't let Snowy go through all that oozy mud. We'll carry him."

SPLODGE! SPLOSH! SLUSH!

Pinocchio walked through the sticky, gurgly mud. He carried Snowy in his arms.

The trio arrived back home. Snowy was spotlessly clean, but Pinocchio was dirty. Geppetto was angry with him, but Jiminy explained, "This time he did something right. He kept Snowy clean so Mrs. Floomis didn't have to bathe him again. For once Pinocchio was thinking of somebody else first."

Jungle Charmer

Mowgli and Baloo were on their way home from a visit to the man-village when they came to a gorge whose bridge, like old London bridge, had fallen down.

"Now we'll have to walk miles out of our way," sighed Mowgli.

"Yeah," Baloo agreed, "unless we fix the bridge somehow."

While they pondered their problem, a
little man came running out of the jungle.
"Help! Help!" he cried. "There is a terrible
tiger chasing me." He screeched to a stop
as he saw Baloo. "Oh!" he gasped and
started to run the other way.

"Wait!" called Mowgli. "Don't go away.
Baloo is a friendly bear." The little man
stopped. "That's more than can be said for
that awful tiger," he moaned.

Baloo looked at Mowgli. "Sounds like
Shere Khan."

The little man
looked around
nervously.
"Why didn't
I become
a tiger tamer
instead of a
snake charmer?"
Mowgli wondered
the same thing.

Just then Baloo noticed a snaky form slithering through a nearby tree. He whispered to Mowgli, "Shere Khan's not the only one looking for a meal around here. Kaa the python looks hungry, too."

Mowgli got an idea. He told the snake charmer, "If you can charm that big snake, I'll show you how we can get across that gorge."

The little man said, "I think I can."

He pulled
a fancy flute
from his belt
and began
to play
a soothing tune.
After a moment
down from
the tree
slipped the
slithery python.

Kaa had a dreamy look in his eyes — he was completely entranced by the music. Baloo almost drifted into a dream, too, but Mowgli nudged him awake.

"Snap out of it, Baloo. We've got important work to do."

Mowgli then told the snake charmer to lure Kaa over to the gorge. When Kaa reached the edge, the little man tootled his flute faster.

Kaa, still in a trance, glided across the chasm. He was barely long enough to bridge the gap.

As soon as Kaa reached the other side he was stretched out, stiff as a piece of pipe. Baloo carefully tested the new "bridge" with his foot.

"Seems sturdy to me," he declared. "All we have to do is keep our balance."

Mowgli warned the charmer, "Don't stop playing until we're all across, or Kaa will go limp."

Baloo started across, followed by the little man and Mowgli. They had no sooner arrived at Kaa's halfway point when who should come sneaking up the trail but Shere Khan. When he spotted Mowgli and the little man, he grinned evilly. "This is my lucky day," he purred. "I'll have both man-cub *and* man for dinner!"

They were all so busy balancing their way across the gorge that they didn't notice Shere Khan sneaking up behind them. "I'll pounce on them when I reach the other side," the tiger thought.

When the three were safely on the other side, the snake charmer stopped playing. Kaa woke up, and tragedy struck!

Kaa went limp. Shere Khan was only halfway across, and they both tumbled into the gorge.

"Yelp!" "Hiss!" "Yeow!"

Baloo, Mowgli and the little man looked over the edge in amazement at the thrashing tangle of snake and tiger far below.

Baloo chuckled, "Looks like someone's dinner plans were upset."

"You're right, papa bear," said Mowgli.

The little man thanked them and went on down the path.

As they continued on their way Mowgli said, "I'm glad I've got a friend like you, Baloo. You'd never let me down."

"Well, Kaa sure let Shere Khan down," laughed the bear. "From the sound of all that yelling and snarling, they're not exactly friendly."

One Thing Leads To Another

Jiminy Cricket jumped up on the table and waved his umbrella at Pinocchio. "When the Blue Fairy gave you the gift of life, she didn't expect you to be so naughty!"

Pinocchio sat on a stool and thought for a minute. "I'm not naughty on purpose," he explained. "I try to be good, but —"

"You upset poor old Geppetto every day," the cricket interrupted. "You must be more thoughtful."

"I do my best," Pinocchio said sincerely. "It seems as though my good ideas turn out badly, that's all."

"Nonsense! Rubbish!" shouted Jiminy. He whacked his umbrella on a book to emphasize what he was saying.

"When things go wrong, you know that I'm always sorry," Pinocchio said. "All right," Jiminy admitted. "I know you'll do better."

Pinocchio clapped his hands and burst into song. "The sun is shining, the bells are ringing! The sky is blue and the birds are singing! Hooray, hooray, for this happy day. Now let's go outside and play."

He threw his arms out and spun around happily, but he didn't see the vase on the workbench.

KER-RASH!

Pinocchio knocked over the vase.

"It's broken," cried Pinocchio. "But I didn't mean to break it, believe me."

Jiminy shook his head and frowned. "Here we go again," he said. "Come on, sweep up the pieces."

Pinocchio ran to get a broom. He started to sweep up the broken vase.

SMASH!

Pinocchio pushed the broom handle through the window behind him. The puppet wailed, "Now look what I've done. I didn't mean to!"

Jiminy sighed. "Let's go outside before you break anything else."

Pinocchio ran out
the front door.
He tripped
on the doorstep.
KER-PLASH!
He fell into
a big mud puddle.

Jiminy looked at the mud-spattered boy and sighed the biggest sigh a little cricket ever sighed. "So it goes," he said, shaking his head. "Now your clothes are all dirty."

"I didn't mean to trip," Pinocchio sputtered as he struggled to his feet. "I'll go inside and clean up."

Geppetto came out of the house to see what had happened. Pinocchio didn't know he was there, and he stepped right on the old man's foot.

"Ye-oww!" yelled Geppetto. "My sore toe."

"Now you've done it," Jiminy said. "You stepped on Geppetto and hurt him."

Large tears filled Pinocchio's eyes. "I didn't mean to step on your sore toe. Honest I didn't."

Geppetto took Pinocchio in his arms. "I know you didn't do it on purpose. There, there. Don't cry. Let me kiss away your tears."

Suddenly there was a flash of light.

"The Blue Fairy!" Jiminy cried.

"Pinocchio," she said to the wooden boy, "since you and Geppetto love each other so much, I want to see both of you happy." She smiled and waved her wand.

"There," she said. "The vase is whole again, and the window is repaired. Pinocchio is clean once more, and Geppetto's aching toe is healed."

As suddenly as the Blue Fairy had appeared, she vanished.

"All's well that ends well," Jiminy announced, "thanks to our Blue Fairy."

A Fish Story

Pinocchio and Jiminy Cricket were fishing by a stream when who should come along but J. Worthington Foulfellow (also known as Honest John) and Gideon the cat. The fox and cat hadn't eaten all day, and Pinocchio's fish looked mighty tempting. Honest John tried to look sincere and the cat tried to look halfway intelligent as they approached Pinocchio.

When the puppet saw Honest John he quickly picked up his basket of fish. Jiminy waved his umbrella and shouted, "Don't steal our fish!"

"Steal? STEAL? Whatever put a thought like that in your head?" sighed the fox. "You're far too clever to let me steal them, but I know where I can *sell* them for you."

Honest John went on, "I have a friend who would give a gold piece for fish like that."

"Gold piece?" Pinocchio exclaimed. He knew he would get only a few pennies for the fish in the market. "In that case, take the fish and sell them for me, please," he said, handing the basket to the fox.

Jiminy knew it was all a big trick, and he tried to stop Pinocchio. But to no avail.

The fox explained, "My friend with the gold coins is very shy. He doesn't like strangers. You wait here and I'll be back."

Pinocchio waited and waited and waited.

At last Pinocchio realized he had been cheated — there had never been any friend, and the fox wanted the fish only for himself.

Pinocchio was furious, and he began searching for Honest John. He found him sitting under a tree and roasting the fish over a fire. Honest John was saying, "I like that lad.

He's my kind of boy. If everybody were like him, our lives would be much easier."

The boy whispered, "You make faces at them, Jiminy. While they are chasing you, I'll get back our fish."

Jiminy screamed and made faces, then went hopping off, with the fox and cat close behind. However, he knew the woodland paths better than Foulfellow and Gideon, and he soon lost them.

Pinocchio and Jiminy went home with the fish (cooked to a turn by the fox). They were happy that at last they had outsmarted J. Worthington Foulfellow and Gideon the cat.

The Present

Jiminy Cricket, as Pinocchio's official conscience, was always asking questions:

"Did you brush your teeth?"

"Did you wash your face?"

"Did you do your homework?"

"Were you a good boy?"

Pinocchio grew tired of Jiminy, but he tried to be patient.

On the day of Betty's birthday party Jiminy was especially active.

Geppetto sent
the puppet
off to the party,
and Jiminy asked,
"Did you kiss
Geppetto goodbye?"

Pinocchio had forgotten, and he shook his head. "No," he said.

As they walked along the street, Jiminy said, "Did you remember to put on your socks?"

Pinocchio looked down and saw that he had neglected to wear his socks.

This time, however, Pinocchio was one up on Jiminy Cricket. He held up the neatly-wrapped package and said, "Did you remember to buy a present for Betty?"

"Golly, Pinocchio's right," Jiminy admitted. He raced along the street to buy a present. He muttered under his breath, "I was so busy telling him what he had forgotten that I forgot to do something myself."

Soon Jiminy had purchased a present, and he continued behind Pinocchio. "Don't walk into that puddle and get your shoes muddy."

SPLOSH!
Jiminy tripped
and fell right
into the puddle.
He was soaked
all over.
Pinocchio
picked him up
and shook water
from his clothes.

He said, "Jiminy, don't you think you should look out for yourself first and me second?"

"Nonsense," Jiminy replied. "It's my job to see that you do the right thing."

A few days after the party Jiminy was
at it again. "Christmas is coming up. Have
you bought Geppetto a present yet?"

Pinocchio was playing ball and didn't
want to worry about a present. Besides, he
was better at remembering presents than
Jiminy! Who had forgotten to get Betty a
birthday gift?

Later Jiminy re-reminded him, but
Pinocchio was sipping hot chocolate by the
fireplace and couldn't be bothered.

Finally it was the week before Christmas. The first snow had fallen, and Pinocchio and his friends were throwing snowballs. Jiminy was trying to tell Pinocchio about Christmas, but the puppet was too busy to listen.

Geppetto was watching them from the door to his workshop. "I'd like to play, too," he smiled, "but my back is too stiff to bend down and make snowballs."

Geppetto went inside to think about a Christmas gift for Pinocchio. He was very poor and was sad because he had no money.

There was no money
to buy anything.
"The only thing
Pinocchio might like
is my old
concertina,"
he decided.
He took it out
and cleaned
and painted it.

As he worked on the concertina, Geppetto said, "I don't like to part with it. It's been like an old and valued friend to me. But nothing is too good for my little Pinocchio." When it shone like new, Geppetto wrapped it and put it on the top shelf of the cupboard.

It was Christmas Eve before Jiminy got Pinocchio's attention long enough to consider a present for Geppetto. Tears came to the puppet's eyes. "I can't get him anything. I have no money." Jiminy was sorely disappointed — he was a failure as a conscience.

"Wait!" said Pinocchio, jumping up. "I know what to get for Geppetto!"

Pinocchio turned to Jiminy. "Remember the other day when Geppetto said he wanted to throw snowballs but couldn't bend over to make them? Well, why don't we make some and give them to him on Christmas morning?"

He ran outside and made half a dozen first-rate snowballs (with lots of loose snow outside for easy spattering when they hit).

He put the snowballs in a box, wrapped it with paper and put it in the cupboard.

He remembered
the Blue Fairy.
"I wish I wouldn't
get anything
for Christmas,
if you could change
the snowballs
into something nice
for Geppetto."

On Christmas morning Geppetto took
down his box and gave it to Pinocchio.
"Thank you," said the puppet, "and my
present to you is also on the cupboard shelf.
Can you reach it for me?"

So it was that Pinocchio opened the box meant for Geppetto and the wood-carver opened the box meant for the puppet.

Pinocchio found his box to be empty. The snowballs had melted in the warm room.

Filled with excitement, Pinocchio told Geppetto of his wish to the Blue Fairy. "If she has taken away my present, then she has put something special in your box," he cried. "Open it and see what is inside."

Geppetto removed the concertina.

By this time Geppetto realized how the presents had been mixed up, but he didn't say anything. There was a lump in his throat, and he couldn't speak.

Instead, he began playing his concertina, and everybody danced.

Jiminy Cricket thought perhaps the gifts had been mixed up, but for once he asked no questions.

After all, it *was* Christmas.